Disney's

WINNIE the POOH'S
SiLLY DaY

by Bruce Talkington

Illustrated by Robbin Cuddy

DiSNEY
PRESS

NEW YORK

Disney's

WINNIE the POOH'S

SiLLY DaY

Rabbit had called a meeting. Everyone in the Hundred-Acre Wood knew that Rabbit didn't call meetings unless something very significant was afoot. To Rabbit, meetings were as important as gravy was to mashed potatoes or honey was to a certain bear of very short legs who was, at that very moment, stumping his way to Rabbit's as quickly as those same very short legs would allow.

Running just as quickly toward the meeting from a quite different direction (and on legs even shorter than Pooh Bear's) was Pooh's good friend Piglet.

And Eeyore, carrying his tail in his mouth so as not to lose it in his hurry, was galloping so rapidly to the gathering (from yet *another* direction) that his back legs would occasionally outdistance his front ones and the donkey would suddenly find

himself running backward. He would then have to stop and get himself sorted out before his frantic journey could continue.

Gopher was scurrying so rapidly through his tunnels in order to reach the meeting place on time that the trees aboveground quaked gently as he jostled their roots in passing.

And high above those trembling treetops, Tigger tore toward the meeting in a series of tremendous bounces.

Meanwhile, Rabbit, at whose house the meeting was to take place, couldn't contain his excitement and was scampering through the woods toward the others to make sure they were all on their way and would not be late.

As a result of this hurrying, scurrying, scampering, galloping, and bouncing, the friends not only were on time for the meeting but were even early! Everyone arrived at a particular crossroads at precisely the same moment, all moving too fast to stop until they'd tumbled head over heels over one another and wound up in a friendly sort of tangle with Tigger on top and Gopher on the bottom while Eeyore's tail drifted down to lay limply across his muzzle.

"I suppose," sniffed Rabbit after they all had untangled themselves and politely dusted off one another's dusty places, "that we can call the meeting to order right here and now so Pooh Bear can get on with his assignment."

Pooh's ears perked up in surprise. "As-SIGN-ment?! I'm not very good at making signs, you know. I'm never quite sure why using a certain letter isn't just as good as using one of the others. And there are so very many to choose from. It's quite confusing."

Rabbit pulled his ears down as if he were going to tie them in a bow beneath his chin. "This has nothing to do with making signs, Pooh Bear," he said. "It has to do with foolishness, which is why we need your help."

Rabbit looked down at Pooh and asked, "You do realize that today is April Fools' Day?"

"Of course," laughed Pooh, delighted to know the right answer for a change. "It's the one day of the year you can look like a fool and not feel unhappy about it."

"Well, I suggest that this year we *not* be fooled," sniffed Rabbit, looking very determined.

"Might be nice for a change," said Tigger with a grin. "We certainly do a stupenderous job o' looking pretty silly the entire rest o' the year."

"You can say that again," agreed Eeyore.

"But today it's someone else's turn, by dinghy!" cackled Gopher.

"Really?" asked Pooh. "Whose turn is it?"

"I think Rabbit means he wants *us* to fool the *April Fool* before *he* fools *us*!" Piglet whispered into Pooh's ear.

"No fooling?" Pooh exclaimed in sudden excitement.

"You don't think that would be impolite, do you, Pooh?" mumbled Eeyore. "I mean, it being his day and all?"

"My goodness, no," laughed Pooh. "Who would enjoy being fooled more than the April Fool? Especially on April Fools' Day!"

Pooh leaned close to his friends and whispered, "How are we going to do it?"

Rabbit whispered back, "You're going to find the April Fool and bring him to my house."

"I am?" asked Pooh in amazement.

"But be careful, Pooh," warned Piglet, giving his friend's hand a tight squeeze. "I've heard that the April Fool can look like anybody!"

"He can?" gasped Pooh.

"Absolutely," whistled Gopher. "That's how he fools ya!"

"Don't worry, Pooh boy," Tigger assured Pooh with a slap on the back. "You'll find 'im. Nobody knows more about foolishness than you do."

As the others hurried off to Rabbit's house to prepare their surprise for the April Fool, Pooh scratched his head furiously with both hands. It didn't help. He hadn't the faintest idea of where to start looking for the April Fool—or what to do with him if he found him.

But it always seemed that the best ideas came when Pooh's head was at its emptiest. All at once Pooh recalled that *fool* rhymed with *pool*. Not one to question sudden inspiration (he wouldn't have known what to ask it, anyway), Pooh proceeded immediately to the largest collection of water in the forest—a quiet pond near the river. As Pooh cautiously crossed from one side of this pool to the other on a series of stepping-stones, the one that happened to be a turtle and not a rock tipped him headfirst into the water.

Sitting on the bottom of the pool, Pooh was, needless to say, thoroughly disappointed. There was not a single fool to be found—only fish, who Pooh knew were not the least bit foolish because they spent so very much of their time in schools.

So Pooh began to look in places that *didn't* rhyme with *fool*.

All he found in a cave were some pesky echoes that loved to make fools of people but were not precisely foolish themselves. They were not precisely anything, really, except a lot of noise, and Pooh, who was very well acquainted with the likes

of Rabbit and Eeyore and Owl, knew that a lot of noise didn't make one foolish ... most of the time. And the bats that all this noise awakened hadn't any interest in fools, only in chasing Pooh away so they could go back to sleep. Pooh managed to escape by plunging back into the pool and sitting on the bottom until the flying grumps returned to their napping.

And when Pooh poked his nose into a certain large hollow tree, he was suddenly swamped by an avalanche of acorns left over from a squirrel's winter storage. Slipping and sliding as the nuts rolled treacherously under his feet, Pooh suddenly found himself sitting down hard in the pool once again.

Exhausted and quite damp, Pooh scrunched his face up into a painful frown because he knew he had some thinking to do and that it wouldn't happen unless his face was pushed into the correct shape for it to take place.

Pooh was positive his friends were right in thinking that he could find the April Fool because foolishness was, after all, something with which he had a great deal of experience. Besides that, he couldn't remember his friends *ever* being wrong. He also couldn't remember what he'd had for breakfast, but that didn't matter because it was time to get to the bottom of things, which was why he'd sat down in the first place.

Pooh sighed and unscrewed his face. "Perhaps I should go to Rabbit's house and ask for help," he said to himself. But he immediately shook his head. "No, that would be foolish. They're busy getting ready to fool the April Fool."

All at once Pooh sat up straight, and a smile lit up his face.

"If it's foolish to go to Rabbit's," Pooh exclaimed, "then that's where the April Fool will be!"

Pooh jumped to his feet and waded to shore. "And I'm sure to be right because, if I do say so myself, that's a pretty foolish idea—so foolish, in fact, that I don't even know what I'm talking about!"

Without wasting another moment, Pooh set off as fast as his dripping legs could carry him.

At Rabbit's house, everyone was ready for the arrival of the April Fool.

Rabbit had set a huge bucket of water over his front door to spill onto the Fool's head when he entered.

Piglet was nearby with a very small, yet very taste-ful, cream pie he'd made from his favorite recipe to toss into the Fool's face.

Off to one side stood Tigger with a huge pepper shaker to sprinkle on the Fool's nose and make him sneeze.

The small rag rug in the entryway was clamped firmly in Eeyore's mouth to be yanked out from under the Fool's feet.

Finally, Gopher was prepared to spill a bag of fluffy feathers that would cling to the damp Fool and cause him to resemble a giant chicken.

The gang was ready for everything except for what happened next.

The front door flew open, and there stood Winnie the Pooh, shouting, "April Fool!" at the top of his voice.

The horrified Rabbit tried to save Pooh from the falling bucket of water but succeeded only in getting it jammed over his own head, which caused him to stumble about blindly.

He bumped into Tigger, who staggered backward and sat in

Piglet's pie, accidentally sprinkling his pepper into Eeyore's nose.

Eeyore, still hanging on to the rug, emitted such a powerful sneeze that it propelled him backward into Gopher, who spilled his feathers all over Piglet as the rug jerked out from under Pooh's feet and set the bear down in the entryway with a loud thump.

After a moment of shocked silence during which the disheveled friends looked at one another in amazement, Pooh finally managed to blurt out, "I was right. The April Fool is here!" Then he looked down at his still-dripping jersey. "But he did seem to be very much out there, too."

Then the laughter began. And it was quite a while before anyone could speak.

Finally, Rabbit, wiping the tears of mirth from his eyes, put his arm around Pooh's shoulders and said, "I think you've discovered the Fool's secret, Pooh Bear!"

Pooh managed to look quite pleased with himself and puzzled at the same time. "I have? What is it?"

"It seems the April Fool is *everywhere*, buddy bear!" hooted Tigger. "An' he looks just like us!"

"And a good thing, too," sighed Pooh.

"Why's that, Pooh Bear?" demanded Piglet, trying to remove a particularly large feather from his very small ear.

"Because then we can all laugh *with* one another—and not *at* anyone," said Pooh. "Or am I being foolish?"

"No, Pooh," said Piglet with a smile. "Not this time."

And the laughter began again and went on and on for a very long time.